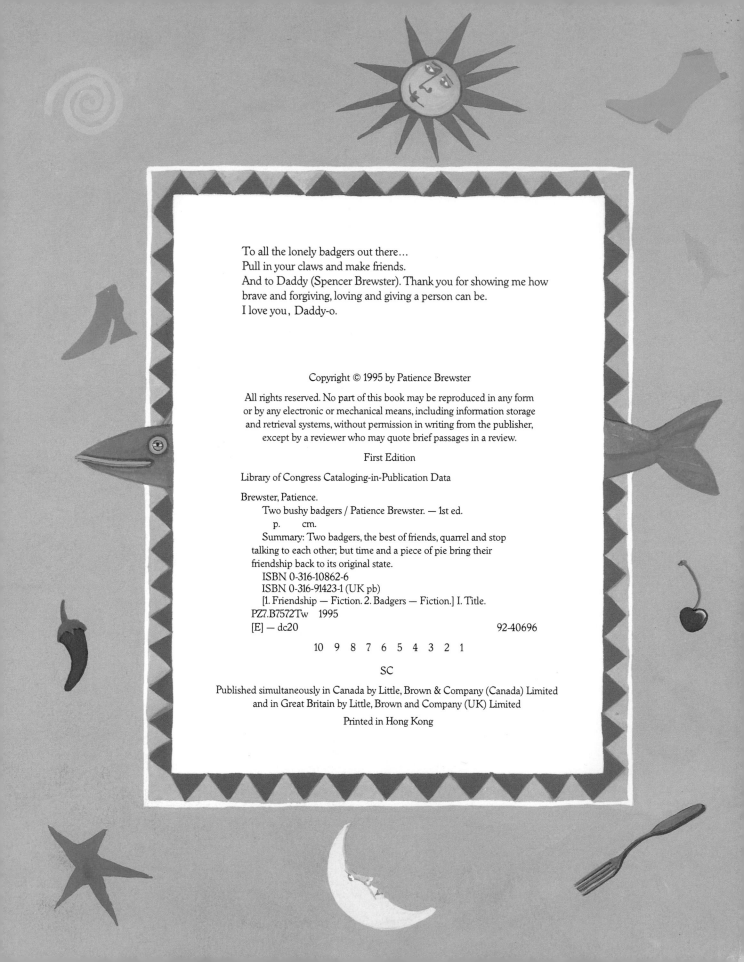

To all the lonely badgers out there…
Pull in your claws and make friends.
And to Daddy (Spencer Brewster). Thank you for showing me how
brave and forgiving, loving and giving a person can be.
I love you, Daddy-o.

First Edition

Library of Congress Cataloging-in-Publication Data

Brewster, Patience.
    Two bushy badgers / Patience Brewster. — 1st ed.
        p.   cm.
    Summary: Two badgers, the best of friends, quarrel and stop
    talking to each other; but time and a piece of pie bring their
    friendship back to its original state.
    ISBN 0-316-10862-6
    ISBN 0-316-91423-1 (UK pb)
    [1. Friendship — Fiction. 2. Badgers — Fiction.] I. Title.
PZ7.B7572Tw   1995
[E] — dc20   92-40696

10   9   8   7   6   5   4   3   2   1

SC

Published simultaneously in Canada by Little, Brown & Company (Canada) Limited
and in Great Britain by Little, Brown and Company (UK) Limited

Printed in Hong Kong

TWO BUSHY BADGERS

PATIENCE BREWSTER

LITTLE, BROWN AND COMPANY

BOSTON · NEW YORK · TORONTO · LONDON

Two fat, bushy badgers
Made a promise to be friends —
Buddies, pals, blood brothers —
Devoted to the end.

They weren't your average badgers,
With snarling, snapping jaws,
No fearsome squinty eyes
Or angry dagger claws.

GROSS

RE-VOLTING

NOT FIT TO BE CALLED BADGERS

E-E-U-U-U-W

DIS-GUS-TING

EM-BARRASSING

These wild, hairy creatures
Whose nature could be mean
Chose a gentle life-style,
Gave up the grouch routine.

These badgers *liked* to share,
To always be polite.
They tried to eat their meals
Together every night.

Till once it got so hot out,
So sticky, thick, and muggy,
The air was like a blanket,
The skeeters drove them buggy.

One badger worked too hard,
And one forgot to eat,
Which made their tempers hot,
Explosive in such heat.

Ollie made some dinner
To help them both unwind,
But when he served it up,
Short Arthur spoke his mind.

Instead of saying, "Thank you,"
He really got quite rude.
He wrinkled up his nose and said,
"I hate this rotten food!"

"WELL, NOW!" said the tall one.
"If the truth be told...
What's rotten is your *feet* —
I see they've grown some mold!"

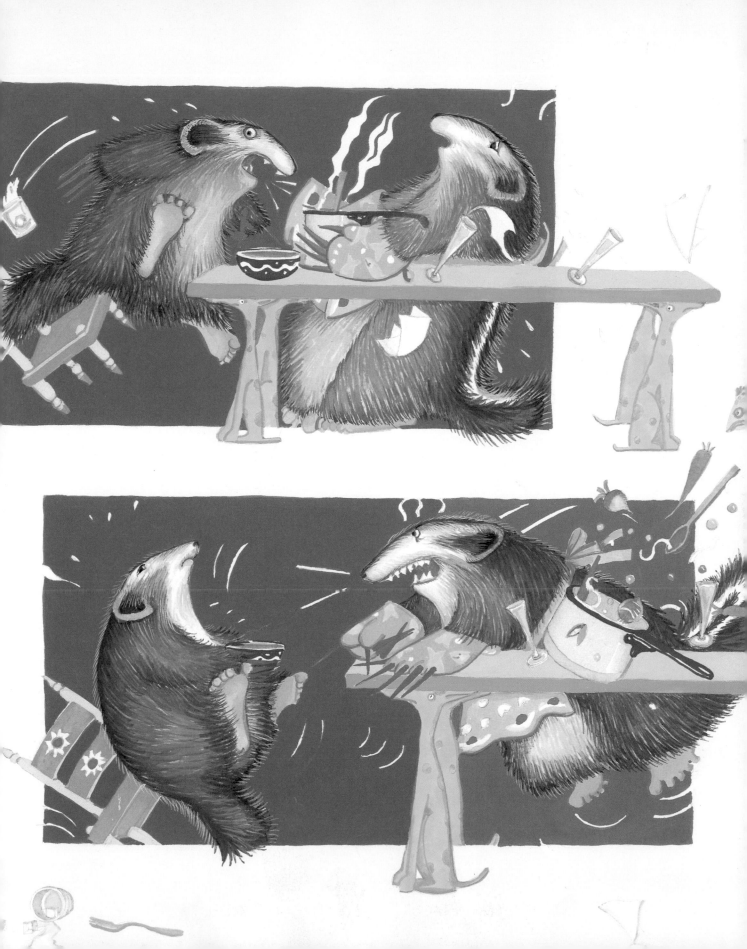

The short one went berserk:
"I hate your wicked peas!
And as for washing tootsies,
I'll do that when I please!"

By now the pair was fuming,
Steam rising from their heads.
They dumped their sizzling dinners
And marched upstairs to bed.

DUMB
DUMB
DUMMY

LUNATIC

TURKEY

IDIOT

RATS

STUPIDO

Each ignored the other
For days and days on end,
Pretending not to miss
His one and only friend.

WICKED MOLDY SMELLY STINKY P.U. ROTTEN FEET

Secretly they wanted
Their pain to disappear
Along with awful words
Still ringing in their ears.

At night they shuffled out
To the old Foot Stomp Café
For single servings hardly touched
Of octopus soufflé.

Then one Thursday evening,
Alone and feeling low,
Each badger watched the sign light up
And flash in neon glow.

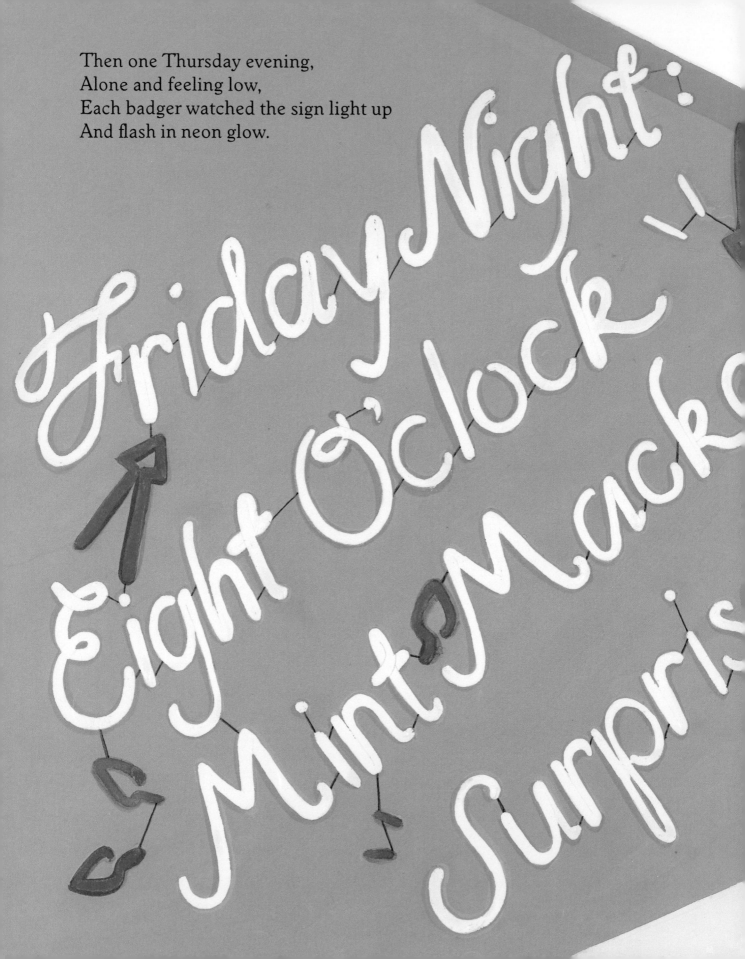

Friday Night:
Eight O'clock
Mint Macke
Surpris

"Friday night, eight o'clock:
Mint Mackerel Surprise —
The brand-new café special —
Come and feast your eyes."

The old Foot Stomp
Was packed that night
With fat raccoons
And ferrets,
Waiting for
The great fish dish
And not inclined
To share it.

Then through swinging
Kitchen doors
The pie came
Like a dream,
All whipped up
With anchovies
And topped with
Pink ice cream.

The dish was so deluxe,
It made the whole crowd hush.
The diners grabbed their forks
And made a massive rush.

Standing back, the badgers
Let everyone pass by,
Till there was nothing left
But half a bite of pie.

Each badger claimed the bite
With fire in his eyes.
The diners stood in shock,
Afraid the fur would fly.

The waitress broke the silence
And rang out, "Hanky, please!"
But it was just too late;
She let go with a...

NEEZe!

The eensy speck of pie
Flew right across the room
And landed with a *plop*
Beside a dirty broom.

The waitress stood there shaking
Behind her ice cream scoops.
About the plop of pie,
All she said was…"Oops."

The badgers, face to face,
Could finally wage their war,

But did they really want
That blob upon the floor?

"The pie looks pretty awful."
(Tall Ollie dared to speak.)
"If you come home for dinner,
I'll *never* mention feet."

"Just look at these," said Arthur.
"My feet are fresh today.
I've found it quite delicious
To wash them every day!"

Cheers came from the Foot Stomp
As the badgers waltzed outside,
Once again best buddies
That nothing would divide.